EARLY ONE MORNING

MEM FOX &
CHRISTINE DAVENIER

Beach Lane Books
New York London Toronto Sydney New Delhi

Love to the wonderful Whitingtons, baby and all!—M. F.

For Valentine and Arthur's baby boy, with all my love—C. D.

BEACH LANE BOOKS • An imprint of Simon & Schuster Children's Publishing Division • 1230 Avenue of the Americas, New York, New York 10020 • Text copyright © 2021 by Mem Fox • Illustrations copyright © 2021 by Christine Davenier • All rights reserved, including the right of reproduction in whole or in part in any form. • BEACH LANE BOOKS is a trademark of Simon & Schuster, Inc. • For information about special discounts for bulk purchases, please contact Simon & Schuster Special Sales at 1-866-506-1949 or business@simonandschuster.com. • The Simon & Schuster Speakers Bureau can bring authors to your live event. For more information or to book an event, contact the Simon & Schuster Speakers Bureau at 1-866-248-3049 or visit our website at www.simonspeakers.com. • The text for this book was set in ITC Galliard. • The illustrations for this book were rendered in pen and ink washes. • Manufactured in China • 1120 SCP • First Edition • 10 9 8 7 6 5 4 3 2 1 • Library of Congress Cataloging-in-Publication Data • Names: Fox, Mem, 1946– author. | Davenier, Christine, illustrator. • Title: Early one morning / Mem Fox ; illustrated by Christine Davenier. • Description: First edition. | New York : Beach Lane Books, [2021] | Audience: Ages 3-8. | Audience: Grades 2-3. | Summary: "A little boy takes a walk to fetch something for his breakfast before sitting down for a meal with his grandmother"—Provided by publisher. • Identifiers: LCCN 2020030059 (print) | LCCN 2020030060 (ebook) | ISBN 9781481401395 (hardcover) | ISBN 9781481401401 (ebook) • Subjects: CYAC: Farm life—Fiction. | Domestic animals—Fiction. | Breakfasts—Fiction. • Classification: LCC PZ7.F8373 Ear 2021 (print) | LCC PZ7.F8373 (ebook) | DDC [E]—dc23 • LC record available at https://lccn.loc.gov/2020030059 • LC ebook record available at https://lccn.loc.gov/2020030060

Early one morning, a little boy went for a walk in search of a couple of things for his breakfast.

He came to a gate . . .

but *gates* don't lay them!

He came to a truck . . .

but *trucks* don't lay them!

He came to a tractor . . .

but *tractors* don't lay them!

So on he walked.

He came to a haystack . . .

but *haystacks* don't lay them!

He came to a cow . . .

but *cows* don't lay them!

Neither do sheep!

(Or even ponies.)

So who *does* lay them?

Well, YOU knew all along . . .

of course!